THE BEDTIME CHRONICLES

LEGEND OF THE DADMAN

Written By
Derek Siskin

Illustrated By
Jamie Sale

To my father, Jay Siskin, the original Dadman,
whose superpowers were his kindness, his laughter, his heart and his
soul, and the undeniable love that he had for his family.

This one's for you pops. Sweet dreams.

- DS

To Jack and Luke, my favorite place is wherever you are.
To my father, my first buddy, who taught me family comes first.

To all the Dadmans, keep doing your thing.

- RA

PREPARE TO RHYME

READ OR RAP

IT'S YO BEDTIME

My name is Benny and that's my sister Mary Lou,

I'm five years old, Mary's eight, and her hair is blue.

This is my bunny, we like to call him Hip-Hop,
he's pretty chill hence the shades and the flip-flops.

My mom is Pam, my dad is Stan – short for Stanley,
and now I've told you 'bout the whole Rimes family.

Anyways, the day is done so before I get all snore-y, you bet your butt I wanna hear a bedtime story.

The Dadman was an extra ordinary guy,
he didn't brag, he didn't boast, he wasn't fly.

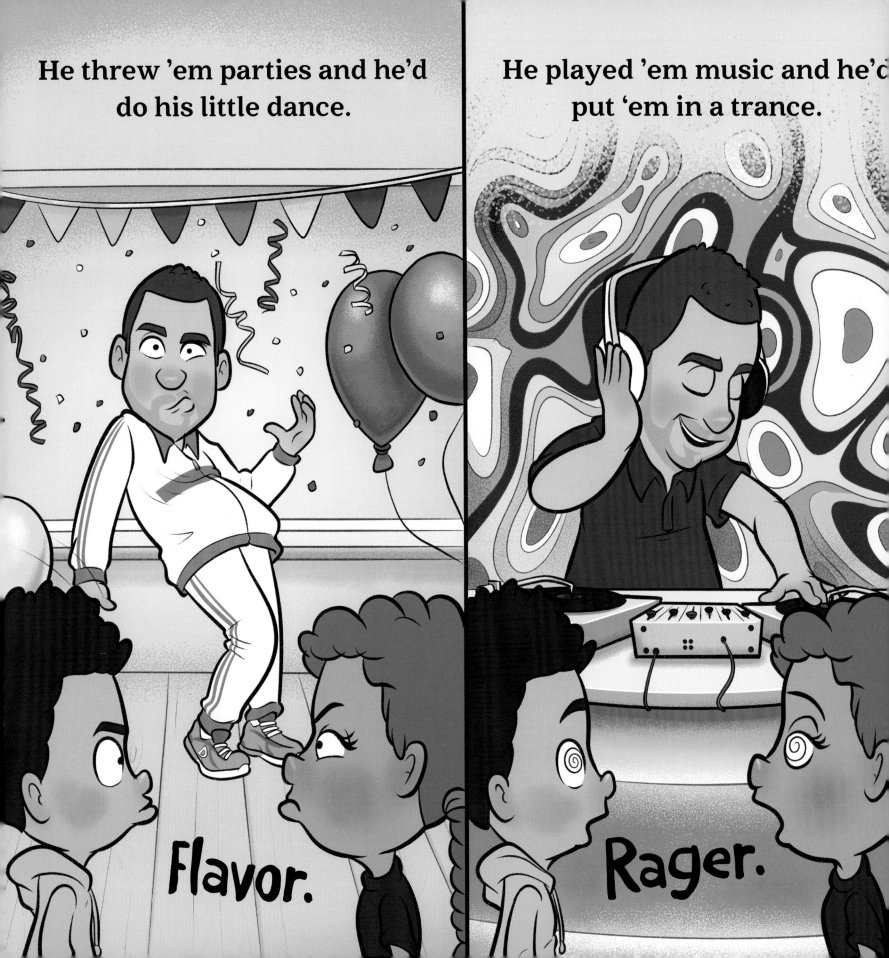

And he did piggyback rides
cause he was strong.
And he could reach high shelves
cause he was long.

Dadman didn't even think
monsters were scary...
cause HE was sweaty,
HE was smelly,
HE WAS HAIRY!

But other times he could relax and be a chill dad.

Could throw a couple burgers on and be a grill dad.

Could fix a toy his kids enjoy
cause he's a drill dad.

Could teach a class in passing gas
cause he's a skilled dad.

Farts and crafts!

And he wore socks with sandals and the same old shorts,
yet somehow managed to be pretty good at sports.
Truth be told, he had what's known as a "dad bod,"
no muscle definition but the perfect flab bod.

He's made of
Play-Doh!

But even Dadman was known to make mistakes.

Like the time he ate all his kids' cupcakes.
Sounds like you.

The point is Dadman wasn't perfect,
he had flaws.
But he stood for a very noble cause.
Doing the best he could
every single day.

To connect.

Lifting people up
in different types of ways.

Respect!

Not quite a hero, but he's super to his fam,
more of a hoagie filled with jelly beans and jam.
As luck would have it,
has a wife whose name is Pam.

Shouts to mom.

And that concludes the
Legend of the Dadman.

He's the bomb!

Now cozy up and get some rest because it's bedtime.

You got it pop - c'mon Hip-Hop,
until the next rhyme.

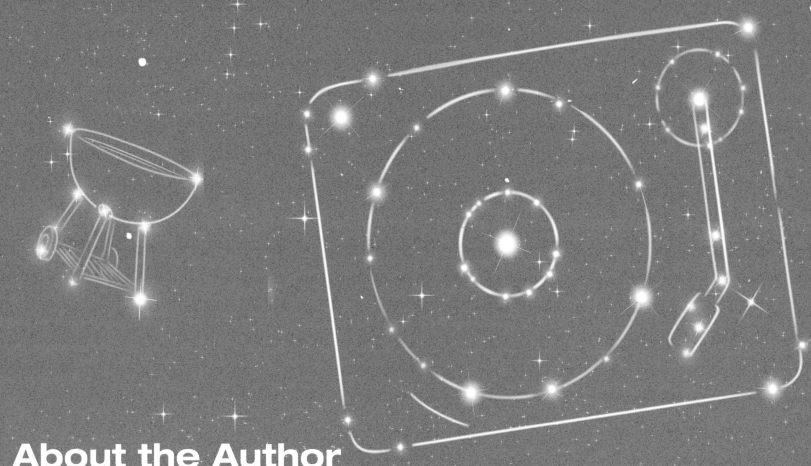

About the Author

Derek Siskin has loved writing, storytelling, humor, and hip-hop music ever since he was a little kid. The Bedtime Chronicles is his first children's book series, allowing him the perfect reason to mix all of that good stuff together. When he's not talking about himself in the third person, Derek lives on Long Island, NY with his wife, Ali, and two sons, Mylo and Freddy.

About the Illustrator

Jamie Sale, since age 4, developed an obsession with drawing characters. An obsession which would later lead him to his path of becoming a cartoon illustrator by trade and being rewarded with amazing projects to work on such as The Bedtime Chronicles. Having young children himself, Jamie's first-hand experience at being a Dadman was vital in capturing the essence of Derek's characters through illustrations.